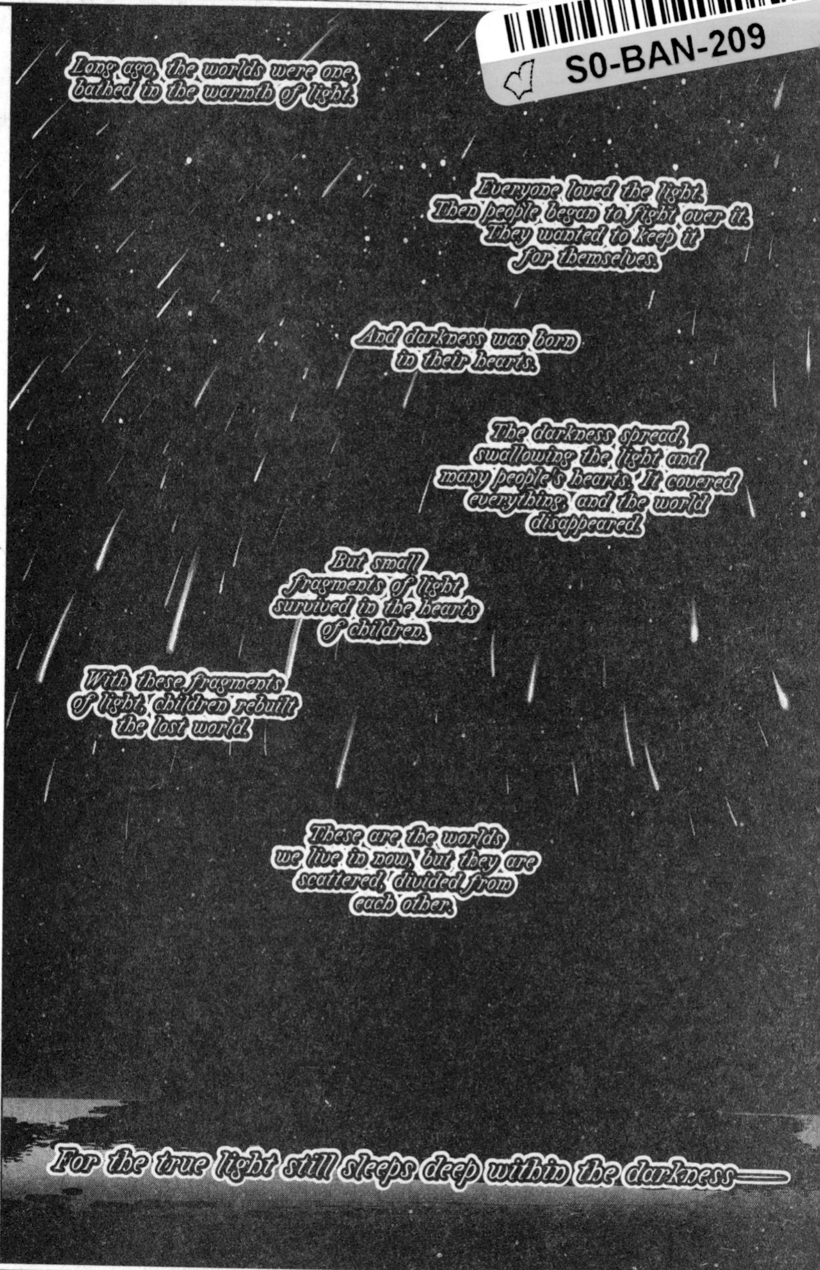

Long ago, the worlds were one, bathed in the warmth of light.

Everyone loved the light. Then people began to fight over it. They wanted to keep it for themselves.

And darkness was born in their hearts.

The darkness spread, swallowing the light and many people's hearts. It covered everything, and the world disappeared.

But small fragments of light survived in the hearts of children.

With these fragments of light, children rebuilt the lost world.

These are the worlds we live in now, but they are scattered, divided from each other.

For the true light still sleeps deep within the darkness—

SHSHHH ———...
SHSHHH ———..
WHO... ARE YOU?
SHSHHH—
WHERE DID YOU COME FROM...?

Episode 1
CALLING

...HRN.
HEY!!
JOLT
GOTCHA!
KAIRI...
KNEW I'D FIND YOU SNOOZING OVER HERE ABOUT NOW...
...SORA!
GLARE
...N-NUH-UH, YOU GOT IT WRONG!

I HEARD SOMEONE CALLING......
...WAS IT... A DREAM—?
WOWWW!!
IT'S ALMOST DOOONE!
OUR RAFT—!!
YEAH... NO THANKS TO YOU GUYS!
YOU TWO'RE ALWAYS SLACKING TOGETHER—!
DON'T TELL ME YOU WERE OFF SHARING A PAOPU FRUIT OR SOMETHING?

DON'T SAY STUFF LIKE THAT, RIKU!
HEY, I WAS ONLY KIDDING.
CAN'T TAKE A JOKE, HUH, SORA?
IS THERE REALLY ANOTHER WORLD...
...AT THE END OF THIS OCEAN?

WE'LL KNOW WHEN WE GET THERE.
KSSHK
KSSHK
I WONDER WHAT IT'LL BE LIKE...
WE'LL FIND OUT WHAT KIND OF WORLD KAIRI CAME FROM...
...AND WE'LL FIND OUT WHY WE'RE HERE...

IF KAIRI HADN'T COME TO THIS ISLAND...
...WE NEVER WOULD HAVE IMAGINED THAT THERE WERE OTHER WORLDS OUT THERE.
WE WOULD'VE LIVED OUT OUR WHOLE LIVES SURROUNDED BY THIS UNCHANGING LANDSCAPE...
HEY!
YOU GUYS!
LOOK WHAT I JUST MADE!
A THALASSA SHELL CHARM!
IN THE OLD DAYS, SAILORS WORE THEM TO ENSURE A SAFE VOYAGE.
IT'S SO WHEREVER WE GO, WE'LL ALWAYS MAKE IT BACK HERE SAFE AND SOUND...
SPLASH
SPLASH
THERE'S NOTHING TO WORRY ABOUT!

C'MON, LET'S GO!
THE THREE OF US ARE GONNA GO SEE THE WORLD!
RIGHT?!
SORA!
HERE.
TOSS
!

IF TWO PEOPLE SHARE THE PAOPU FRUIT, THEIR DESTINIES BECOME INTERTWINED.
THEY'LL REMAIN A PART OF EACH OTHER'S LIVES, NO MATTER WHAT.
YOU MIGHT WANNA TRY IT OUT BEFORE WE SET SAIL, Y'KNOW?
...HUH?!
IF YOU'RE NOT GONNA, HOW 'BOUT I GIVE IT A SHOT?
...HUNH?!
WAIT A —!
HEY, YOU TWO! LET'S HEAD BACK!
SEE YA.
ACK...!
...GOOD GRIEF!
...WHO DOES HE THINK HE IS—?!
So much to do, so little time.

There's no turning back now.
The door is still shut—
But take your time. Don't be afraid.
OH NOOO!!!!!
WADDLE WADDLE WADDLE

THE KING —!
WADDLE
WADDLE
WADDLE
WADDLE
THE KING —!!!
WADDLE
WADDLE
WADDLE
CAPTAIN GOOFY!
SCREEE
EECH
MMM, NYUM...
A-HYUCK...
WAKE UUUP!!!!
ZAAAA
A-HYIPE!
AP!
OKAY, GOOFY... STAY CALM AND LISTEN UP......!!
A-HYUCK!
SIZZLE SIZZLE
IT'S ABOUT THE KING...
THE KING?
NOW, WE'VE GOT A PROBLEM, GOOFY! BUT DON'T TELL ANYONE—
...NO, SHHH!
WE DON'T WANT TO CAUSE A PANIC!
DONALD, WHAT'S ALL THE COMMOTION?
A-HYUCK.

THE KING IS GONE?!
OH MY...
WHEN I WENT TO GREET HIM THIS MORNING, HE HAD ALREADY...
PLUTO HAD THIS LETTER IN HIS MOUTH.
I TOOK THE LIBERTY OF FIXING UP THE BITS HE SMUDGED WITH HIS DROOL.
WE DIDN'T NEED TO KNOW THAT!
OH MY...
DONALD—
SORRY TO RUSH OFF WITHOUT SAYIN' GOOD-BYE.
BUT BIG TROUBLE'S A-BREWIN', AND THERE'S NO TIME TO LOSE. I HAD TO LEAVE AT ONCE—

THE STARS HAVE BEEN BLINKIN' OUT ONE BY ONE, AND THAT MEANS DISASTER CAN'T BE FAR BEHIND.
I HATE TO LEAVE YOU ALL, BUT I'VE GOTTA GO LOOK INTO IT.
......
PAOPU FRUIT, HUH ...?
BLUUUSH
...BLEH!
WHAT A FAIRY TALE!
WHAP
AS KING, I HAVE A FAVOR TO ASK OF YOU AND GOOFY.
G'NIGHT!
FWUMP
THERE'S SOMEONE OUT THERE WHO HOLDS THE "KEY" TO ALL THIS—THE KEY TO OUR SURVIVAL. SO I WANT YOU AND GOOFY TO FIND HIM AND STICK WITH HIM! GOT IT?

WE NEED THAT KEY—
"SO GO TO TRAVERSE TOWN AND FIND THE MAN CALLED LEON..."
TRAVERSE TOWN...
THAT'S ANOTHER WORLD...!!
OH DEAR! WHAT COULD THIS MEAN ...?!
SHSHSHHH

THE DOOR IS OPENING...

Episode 2
INVADERS

SORAAA?
FSSSHHH...
WHERE ARE YOOOU?
ARGH!
POUT
WE STILL HAVE TO GET READY TO SET SAIL TOMORROW AND EVERYTHING...

THIS IS OUR SECRET PLACE— JUST ME AND RIKU!

NO ONE ELSE'S S'POSED TO COME IN HERE, SEE!
BUT I'M MAKING AN EXCEPTION FOR YOU, KAIRI!
WHOOOA, SO COOL!
BEFORE WE GO...
SCRITCH..
SCRITCH
SCRITCH
SCRITCH...
SCRI-
THIS WORLD HAS BEEN CONNECTED...

HIDE
...WHO —?!
ARE YOU?!
TIED TO THE DARKNESS, SOON TO BE COMPLETELY ECLIPSED...
JUST LIKE THE WORLDS THAT HAVE VANISHED BEFORE IT......
...WHA —?!
WHAT ARE YOU TALKING ABOUT?
YOU'RE NOT MAKING ANY SENSE...
!
......
YOU...
YOU DO NOT YET KNOW WHAT LIES BEYOND THE DOOR......
WHERE DID YOU COME FROM......?
YES...YOU DO NOT YET KNOW ANYTHING—

SORA?
MARCH MARCH MARCH
WHAT ARE YOU DOING HERE?
...AH!
EEEEEEP!
OH, NOTHIN'! NOTHIN' AT ALL!
L- LET'S GO!
HUH?! WHAT? WHAT IS IT? HEY!
WE HAVE TO GET READY FOR TOMORR—
I KNOW, I KNOW! LOOK, MUSHROOMS! I GOT US MUSHROOMS!
HE'S GONE —?!
THAT WAS KINDA CREEPY......
OKAY, MAKE SURE YOU TWO WAKE UP ON TIME TOMORROW!
YEAH!
'NIGHT!

SWIM RING, BEACH BALL...
RUMBLE RUMBLE...
...BEACH UMBRELLA, OH! MY SWIM TRUNKS, AND...
HN?
URK!
THOSE WERE RIKU AND KAIRI'S BOATS.
RUMBLE RUMBLE...
ARE THEY HERE TOO?
FLASH
RUMBLE RUMBLE...
IT'S ALL OVER IF OUR RAFT GETS WASHED AWAY!

!
RIKU!
FLASH
WHERE'S KAIRI? I THOUGHT SHE WAS WITH YOU!
RUMBLE RUMBLE
RI...
FOOM
RIKU?!

Episode 3
LIGHT IN THE HAND

SORA...
COME... WITH ME.
?!!
CLAMP
CLAMP
DON'T WORRY. KAIRI'S COMING TOO...
DON'T FEAR THE DARKNESS, SORA...
......
...RI...KU.
WHY......?

THERE'S NOTHING HERE—
IT'S PITCH BLACK.

!

KAIRI?!
GLOW
SO...RA...
WHOOSH

WHOOOOM
!!
KAIRI!!!!
SSS

RRRUSH
WAH!
FWOOOOM
!!
Don't be afraid.
!
IT'S THAT VOICE AGAIN—!
FLASH
?!!
You hold the mightiest weapon of all.—

ゴォオオオ
VOOOOSH
VWMM VWMM
VWMM
BE CAREFUL, BOTH OF YOU...
JIMINY CRICKET, AT YOUR SERVICE!
HOPPITY
GET OFFA MY HEAD!!
SHOO! SHOO!
OH, BEGGIN' YOUR PARDON!
WE'LL BE FINE.
FWIP
AND WE WILL...
...BRING BACK THE KING SAFE AND SOUND. COUNT ON IT—!!
PLEASE DON'T WORRY, YOUR MAJESTY!
BUH-BYE ~!

PLUTO

Episode 4
A GIANT SHADOW

A KEY?!
...OR IS IT...A SWORD?
—The Keyblade.
The power that sleeps within you—
KEYBLADE—
CRACK

—!!

YEOW!
THUD
RUMBLE
OWWW...
RUMBLE
......D'WHA?!
RUMBLE
RUMBLE
RUMBLE
RUMBLE

RUMBLE
RUMBLE
RUMBLE
RUMBLE
RUMBLE
...HUH?
WHA-WHA-
WHAAAT??
VWOOM
VWOOM
CHWNG

STOMP
!
Don't be afraid.
SKSH
GULP
SQUIRM
SQUIRM
...
SQUIRM
...I GUESS... I GOTTA FIGHT...
...I DON'T KNOW WHAT'S GOING ON, BUT...

FWOOSH
BWOOSH
TAKE THIS!
LOOOM
DON'T MESS WITH ME! I'VE BEEN SWORD-FIGHTING WITH RIKU FOR AGES!
THERE'S NO END TO THESE LITTLE CREEPS—
I GOTTA GET THE BIG ONE...!!
GWOOM
BOOOOM
URGH!

AREN'T YOU A LITTLE TOO BIG ...?!!
STOP POSING...
WHAT DO I DO? WHAT DO I...?
FLEX
WHEN YOU ENCOUNTER A GIANT ENEMY, AIM FOR THE EYES.
NO ONE CAN TOUGHEN ONE'S EYES...
EXCERPT FROM LIFE AND DEATH BATTLE WITH A BENGAL TIGER BY BOXER SHIHOROU OKADA
GWOOM
WHO'S THAT?
DASH
DASH
DASH DASH
DASH
AH!
YOUR FACE IS WIDE OPENNN!!!

Episode 5
CAST ASHORE

HOW'S THAT?!!
WOBBLE...
WHAM
SKSH!
WANT ONE MORE...?
HERE YA—
?!
CRACK CRACK CRACK

WHOOM
!!!!

WAH...!
CLIIING
URK...!
HNGH... GUH...

FLASH
GAWRSH?!
DONALD!
LOOK! A STAR'S GOIN' OUT......
...!!
WHFF

......
WE GOTTA FIND "THE ONE WHO HOLDS THE KEY" RIGHT AWAY—
LET'S HURRY!
?
HUH? WHERE'S PLUTO?
SNIFF SNIFF
FIRST, HE TAGS ALONG, AND THEN HE DISAPPEARS —!
DASH
SNIFF SNIFF
SNIFF SNIFF
!
......UHNN.

LICK!
WAAH?!!
PANT
PANT
PANT
WH-WHAT THE—?
HUH...? A DOG?!
...HEY, WAIT A MINUTE!

WHAT IS THIS PLACE...?

I GOT SUCKED UP WITH THAT GIANT THING, AND THEN...
WHERE...... AM I...?!
HE'S HERE...
......
GUESS YOU CAN'T TELL ME, HUH...?
PANT PANT PANT
SCRITCH SCRITCH
DASH
HEY! WAIT!
...AW, MAN.
...THE "KEY" BEARER.

Episode 6
TRAVERSE TOWN

......
WHAT A WEIRD TOWN...
HI THERE, LITTLE MAN.
FIRST TIME IN TRAVERSE TOWN?
WHY DON'T YOU LET BIG SIS HERE SHOW YOU AROUND?♡
??!!
N-N-NO THANKS!
AWW, HEE-HEE-HEE. DON'T BE SHY.
IT'S NOT THAT...!
WSH
WHOOS
?!
CLANK
CLANK
CLANK

ZHNK
H-HER HEART?!
THUD
SPARKLE
SPARKLE
SPARKLE
SPARKLE
SHATTER
WSHHHH...
!!
SHE'S DISAPPEARING?!
CLANK CLANK
WHA—
JOLT...
WHAT IS THIS GUY ......?!
GROWL
WHOOOA!!!!
SLAM
IT'S THOSE CREATURES FROM THE ISLAND...!

HFF!
HFF!
HEY THERE, WHAT CAN I DO YA FOR?
...AW.
TSK, TSK.
YOU DON'T LOOK LIKE A CUSTOMER, KIDDO......
AND IF YOU AIN'T A CUSTOMER, GET OUT!
SHOCK
BAM
BAM
!!
...THEM AGAIN, HUH?
TCH!
ROTTEN HEARTLESS ......
OUTTA MY WAY.
DON'T! IF YOU OPEN THE DOOR NOW—
CID CANNON
SNAP

YOU'RE BAD FOR BUSINESS, CREEPS!!!!!
BOOM
BOOM
BOOM
BOOM
WHOOSH...
RUSTLE
...THERE WE GO.
SHUT
HEY KID, YOU NEW 'ROUND HERE...?
I'M NOT A KID! AND THE NAME'S SORA.
CLUNK
OKAY, OKAY, SIMMER DOWN. NICE TO MEET YA, SORA.
THOSE HEARTLESS YOU SAW'RE MONSTERS THAT EAT PEOPLE'S HEARTS.
WHERE'D YOU COME FROM?
HAVEN'T SEEN 'EM HERE IN THE FIRST DISTRICT FOR A WHILE...

THEY MUST'VE FOUND SOMETHING HERE THAT REALLY MADE THEIR MOUTHS WATER...
HUNH?!
GRAMPS?!
IS THIS REALLY ANOTHER WORLD?
HEY! GRAMPS!
I WAS ON THE ISLAND......
NEXT THING I KNOW, I'M IN THIS TOWN.
AND I GOT SPLIT UP FROM MY FRIENDS......
...RIKU...
...AND KAIRI......!
WELL, THIS HERE'S TRAVERSE TOWN.
IT'S WHERE PEOPLE END UP WHEN THEY LOSE THE PLACES THEY CALL HOME.
YOUR FRIENDS OUGHTA BE HERE TOO.
TAKE A LOOK AROUND TOWN FOR 'EM.
...'KAY.
HERE, THINK FAST!
SMACK
!

EAT THAT AND GET YOUR CHIN UP.
IT'S A LEFTOVER SOMEONE GAVE ME, BUT...
IF YOU EVER RUN INTO TROUBLE, YOU COME TO ME. I'LL LOOK OUT FOR YOU.
HALF-EATEN
GRAMPS...
AND DON'T CALL ME GRAMPS!
THE NAME'S CID!
BAM
THANKS, GRAMPS!
IT'S CID!
SKSH
ACCESSORY
THEY'LL KEEP ON COMING AFTER YOU.
AS LONG AS YOU WIELD THE KEYBLADE!

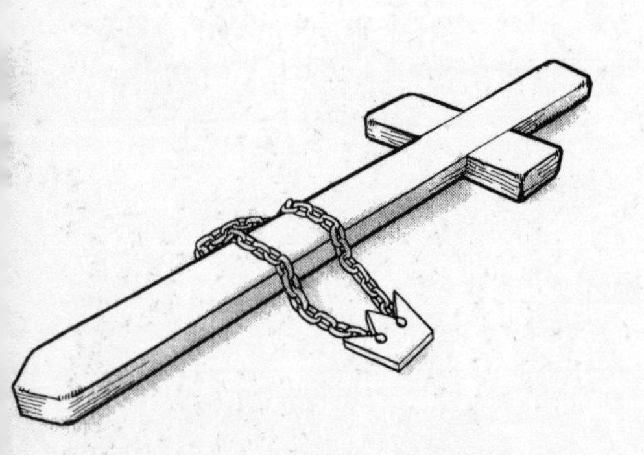

Episode 7
THE MAN CALLED LEON

SORRY, BUT...
...I'M GONNA HAVE TO ASK YOU TO TAKE A LITTLE NAP.
SWFOO
HUH?
WHOOSH
THUD...
YOU OKAY?

...AH.
DAAAZE
KAIRI...?!
KAIRI? WHO'S THAT?
I'M YUFFIE!
!
I THINK YOU MIGHT'VE OVERDONE IT, SQUALL.
KA-CHAK
THAT'S LEON!

MISTER LEEEOOON~!
WHERE ARE YOOOOU~?!

GAWRSH, HE SURE IS HARD TO FIND...
THIS TOWN'S TOO DARN HUGE!
IF'N WE DON'T HURRY, WE WON'T FIND THE "KEY," NEITHER!
I KNOW THAT!
THE "KEYBLADE" YOU POSSESS—
THAT'S WHAT THE HEARTLESS ARE LOOKING FOR.
WE HAD TO CONCEAL YOUR "HEART" TO SHAKE THEM OFF YOUR TRAIL...
H-HEY, HANG ON!
WHY DON'T YOU START MAKING SENSE! WHAT'S GOING ON H—
CRASH
!
GRR! THEY'VE ALREADY SNIFFED YOU OUT, HUH...
BAM
LEON!
YUFFIE, GO!
SORRY, YOUR EXPLANATION'LL HAVE TO WAIT. FOLLOW ME!
WHA—?! H-HEY!

TMP
THERE'RE SO MANY...
THERE MUST BE A BOSS SOMEWHERE.
LET'S GO!
DON'T BOTHER WITH THE SMALL FRY.
EASY FOR YOU TO SAY ...!
WHOA......
DASH
AH! ACK! WAIT...
HELLLP ~~~~!!
LET'S GO GET 'EM, GOOFY!
SCRAPE
SCRAPE
I'MA TRYIN', DONALD, BUT...
A-HYUCK!
EH?
WAK! WHERE D'YOU THINK YOU'RE GOING?!
GAWRSH~! I'M FALLIN'!
UMBLE

!

OWWW.
THE "KEY"!!

RUMBLE..!
RUMBLE
RUMBLE
HUH?! THE WALL'S ...!
?
?!
GLINT
KABOOM
!!
WHWHOMP
CLANK
WHOMP
JANK
WHOMP

BZZT BZZT
BZZT

A-HYUCK!!
CLANG
YIPES...
NOT AGAIN
.......!
GRIP...
WHOOM

WE'LL BACK YOU UP!
SO LET'S FIGHT HIM TOGETHER!
LANK
ZAAAP
WHIZ
UGH ...!
CURE!!!!
GLOO
OOW
THANKS!!

HERE WE GO —!!
JERK
JERK
!!
THIS IS IIIT!!

KACRASH
HINE...

!
TMP
TMP
WOW! NOT TOO SHABBY.

SO YOU WERE LOOKING FOR ME......?

THEY TOO HAVE BEEN SEEKING THE WIELDER OF THE KEY-BLADE.

HEY, WHY DON'T YOU COME WITH US? WE CAN GO TO OTHER WORLDS IN OUR VESSEL.

......
I WONDER IF I COULD FIND RIKU AND KAIRI—
OF COURSE!

YOU SURE?
THAT'S GREAT, A-HYUCK
PSST PSST
WHO KNOWS?
I DO KNOW THAT WE NEED HIM TO FIND THE KING...!

SORA, GO WITH THEM.

ESPECIALLY IF YOU WANT TO FIND YOUR FRIENDS.

......
YEAH... I GUESS...

TSK, TSK, TSK.
BUT YOU CAN'T COME ALONG LOOKING LIKE THAT!
SMILE!!
BEAM
NO FROWNING! NO SAD FACE. OKAY?
OUR SHIP RUNS ON HAPPY FACES!
HAPPY FACES......
A-YUP! YA GOTTA LOOK FUNNY, LIKE US!
A-HYUCK!
L-LIKE... THIS?
GRIN
WAH! HA! HA! HA!
THAT'S ONE FUNNY FACE!
EH... HEH-HEH.

...OKAY, I'LL GO WITH YOU GUYS!
SO YOU'LL LET ME ON YOUR SHIP?
I'M DONALD DUCK.
NAME'S GOOFY.
I'M SORA.

CLAMP
ALL FOR ONE, AND ONE FOR ALL!

WAX

Episode 8
PLOT

HEY NOW, THAT LITTLE SQUIRT TOOK DOWN THAT GIANT HEARTLESS...

SUCH IS THE POWER OF THE KEYBLADE! THE CHILD'S STRENGTH IS NOT HIS OWN...

WHY DON'T WE TURN HIM INTO A HEARTLESS? THAT'LL SETTLE THINGS QUICK ENOUGH...

AND THE BRAT'S FRIENDS ARE THE LACKEYS OF THE "KING."
THEY'RE ALL BILGE RATS BY THE LOOK OF THEM!
YOU'RE NO PRIZE YOURSELF, OLD BOY!
SHUT UP!! WHY, YOU...
ENOUGH.
THE KEYBLADE HAS CHOSEN HIM...
WILL IT BE HE WHO CONQUERS THE DARKNESS?
OR— WILL THE DARKNESS SWALLOW HIM...?

EITHER WAY, HE MAY PROVE QUITE USEFUL.
HA-HA-HA...
OKAY! LET'S GET GOING!!
WHERE'S THE SHIP? THE PORT?
HOLD IT, SORA.
WE'RE GONNA BE GOING TO LOTS OF DIFFERENT PLACES...
SHHH!
...BUT YOU CAN'T TELL ANYONE THAT WE'RE TRAVELING FROM ANOTHER WORLD!
?
WHY NOT?

WE GOTTA PROTECT THE WORLD BORDER!
A-HYUCK.
WAK! THE "ORDER"!
RIGHT.
BUT THAT ORDER IS BEING DISRUPTED...
...BECAUSE OF THE HEARTLESS.
WHAT ARE THEY, ANYWAY?
HEARTLESS... THOSE WITHOUT HEARTS.
RUSTLE
A RESEARCHER NAMED ANSEM FILED A REPORT ON THE HEARTLESS.
I THINK IT MIGHT HELP SOLVE THE MYSTERY, BUT...
...THE REPORT IS SCATTERED EVERYWHERE, AND WE CAN'T FIND IT ALL.

WHAT DO YOU MEAN, "EVERY-WHERE"?
I MEAN TO DIFFERENT WORLDS!
GAWRSH! THAT MEANS THE KING—
RIGHT.
HE MIGHT HAVE GONE LOOKING FOR THAT REPORT!

THE HEARTLESS FEED OFF THE DARKNESS IN PEOPLE'S HEARTS.
WATCH YOURSELF.

THERE IS DARKNESS IN EVERY HEART.

WHERE...
...AM I?

Episode 9
BLAST OFF!

WHOOOOSH

INSIDE THE GUMMI SHIP
HUMM
HUMM
COCK PIT
WOW!
BIGGER'N IT LOOKS, A-HYUCK.
HUMM
HUMM
WELCOME TO OUR GUMMI SHIP!

WOW, LOOK AT THIS!!
WHOO-HOO!
WANDER WANDER
FIDDLE FIDDLE
CHECK THIS OUT! COOL!
WHACK
THAT'S ENOUGH!!!
WILL YOU STOP TOUCHING EVERYTHING YOU SEE?!
WHA—?
HUH?
FUME
WE JUST CLEANED THIS PLACE UP, AND NOW YOU'RE GETTING IT ALL DIRTY!
DOWN HERE!!
YEAH, COME ON.
THOSE PIP-SQUEAKS ARE CHIP 'N' DALE.
HEY! DON'T CALL US "PIP-SQUEAKS"!
THEY'RE THE SHIP'S MECHANICS.
NICE TO MEET YOU!
OKAY, OKAY!
TAKE OFF YOUR SHOES WHEN YOU ENTER THE COCKPIT!

WELCOME ABOARD! I'M JIMINY CRICKET, CAPTAIN OF THIS SHIP!
EVERYBODY READY?
TUG
FASTEN YOUR SEATBELTS.
TAKE THE ENGINE TO FULL THROTTLE!
AYE-AYE, SIR!
BLAST OFF!!!
WHOOOOSH
ZOOOOM
WHOA...!
SORA!
MOTION SICK
TAKE A LOOK OUTSIDE.

AMAZING...!
I WISH RIKU AND KAIRI COULD SEE THIS...

HERE WE ARE!
ALREADY?
LOOK RIGHT, THEN LEFT...
I'M SO EXCITED!
EXCITED
EXCITED
EXCITED
HEY, YOU CAN'T JUST JUMP OUT OF THE SHIP!
DOWN?
CAREFUL!
THAT'S RIGHT.
GAWRSH!
HEY, YOU GUYS, LOOK DOWN!
WONDERLAND!

WAAAAAH!
OUCH...
A-HYUCK!
—HOW COME WE'RE ALWAYS FALLIN' ON OUR BEHINDS?
BE QUIET!
OH, MY FUR AND WHISKERS!!
SQUISH
I'M LATE, I'M LATE, I'M LATE!
THE QUEEN WILL HAVE MY HEAD FOR THIS!
WHAT THE—?
LET'S FOLLOW HIM!

Episode 10
KANGAROO COURT

WAIT!!
STAMP
STAMP
THAT DARN RABBIT...
BAM
HUH?
HE'S GONE!
GLARE
GLARE
WHERE'D HE GO?
HEY!!
I'M OVERDUE! I'M REALLY IN A STEW! NO TIME TO SAY GOOD-BYE, HELLO! I'M LATE, I'M LATE, I'M LATE!
HFF!
SCAMPER SCAMPER
SCAMPER SCAMPER
HFF!
HAAH!

SHUT
WHAT?
HOW'D HE GET SO SMALL??
THIS DOOR'S TINY!
HUH?
NO, YOU'RE SIMPLY TOO BIG.
DRINK FROM THAT BOTTLE, AND GO ON YOUR WAY.
I'M TIRED AND SLEEPY.
THE DOOR'S TALKING!
A-HYUCK, HI THERE!
BOTTLE?
YOU MEAN THIS?
DRINK ME

SHRIIIINK
WOW!
OTHER WORLDS ARE JUST FULL OF WONDERS!
COOL!
HMM...
TOO MANY WONDERS, IF YOU ASK ME.
OKAY.
KA-CHAK
LET'S... HUH?
WE REALLY DID GET SMALL!
HEY, LET US THROUGH.
ZZZ...
HEY, WAKE UP!
SORA, THIS WAY!
I THINK WE CAN GET THROUGH THIS HOLE.
OH BROTHER...

PWEE PWEET
PWEE PWEE
PWEE PRWAAH
AHEM!
COURT IS NOW IN SESSION!

THIS GIRL IS THE CULPRIT! THERE'S NO DOUBT ABOUT IT!
FWSH FWSH...
AND DO YOU KNOW WHY...?
BECAUSE I SAY SO! THAT'S WHY!
THAT IS UTTERLY UNFAIR!
YOU MAY BE THE QUEEN...
FLUSTER FLUSTER
PANIC PANIC
...BUT THAT DOESN'T GIVE YOU THE RIGHT TO BE SO...SO MEAN!
SILENCE!!
WHAT'S GOING ON?
YOU DARE DEFY ME?!
GUILTY AS CHARGED!!
NO...
I'VE DONE ABSOLUTELY NOTHING WRONG!
FOR THE CRIME OF THE ATTEMPTED THEFT OF THE QUEEN'S HEART!

HEART?
HEY, WE HAVE TO HELP HER!
WELL...
NO!
IF WE DO THAT, WE'D BE MEDDLING WITH THEIR WORLD.
AND THAT'S AGAINST THE RULES.
BUT...
OFF WITH HER HEAD!!
!
OH PLEASE!!
HOLD IT RIGHT THERE!!!
OH NO...

Episode 11
FIND THE EVIDENCE!

WHO ARE YOU?!
HOW DARE YOU INTERFERE WITH MY COURT...
...YOU FOOLS?!
WAIT A MINUTE...
WE KNOW WHO THE REAL CULPRIT IS!

YEAH, THE HEARTLE—
MMPH!
IF YOU SAY THAT NAME, THEN WE'D REALLY BE MEDDLING!
WE HAVE TO KEEP THE HEARTLESS A SECRET!
NONSENSE.
HAVE YOU ANY PROOF?
WELL...
UMM...

!
CLANK
VERY WELL... BRING ME THE PROOF OF HER INNOCENCE...
...OR IT'S OFF WITH ALL OF YOUR HEADS!
TILL THEN... COURT IS ADJOURNED!
WHACK!

JUST YOU WAIT! WE'LL FIND WHO REALLY DID THIS!
THE CHESHIRE CAT I MET IN THE WOODS MAY KNOW SOMETHING.
BUT BE CAREFUL—
BUT WHERE CAN WE FIND EVIDENCE?
SHFF
!
SCRAM!
YOU MAY NOT SPEAK WITH THE DEFENDANT!
LET'S TELL THE QUEEN THAT THE HEARTLESS DID IT.
WE'VE DONE PLENTY OF MUDDLIN' ALREADY ANYWAY.
THAT'S "MEDDLING"! AND NO!!

EVERYONE HAS ONLY EVER LIVED IN THEIR OWN, SINGLE WORLD.
WE'D JUST CONFUSE EVERYTHING. THAT'S WHY WE HAVE TO KEEP IT A SECRET.
YOU THINK SO?
WELL, IT'S NOT NECESSARILY TRUE THAT YOU CAN'T SAY THAT THAT'S UNTRUE.
BUT THE CHESHIRE CAT KNOWS EVERYTHING.
ALL YOU HAVE TO DO IS NOT GET CONFUSED.
CHESHIRE CAT!
HERE YOU GO!
BONK
!

BUT CAN YOU REALLY TRUST ME?
I TRUST YOU'LL DECIDE.
SHHH...
THE EVIDENCE YOU'RE LOOKING FOR IS IN THAT BOX.
...OR IS IT?

HE'S GONE!

WHAT'S IN HERE?
I DON'T TRUST HIM.

IT'S A HEART-LESS!
WHOOSH...
STOP!!
?!!

!!
POOF!

YOUR MAJESTY, HE'S THE EVIDENCE!
WHAT! WHO IS THAT?!
CLATTER
WHY, YOU—!
LOOK OUT!
NO!
BAM
GRRR...
DO YOU SEE?!
NOW DO YOU SEE THAT ALICE IS INNOCENT?
LET HER GO!
...ALICE?!
SHFF!
CRANK CRANK
NOW, A-HYUCK!
HEY, YOU CAN'T LOWER THE—
CRANK CRANK CRANK

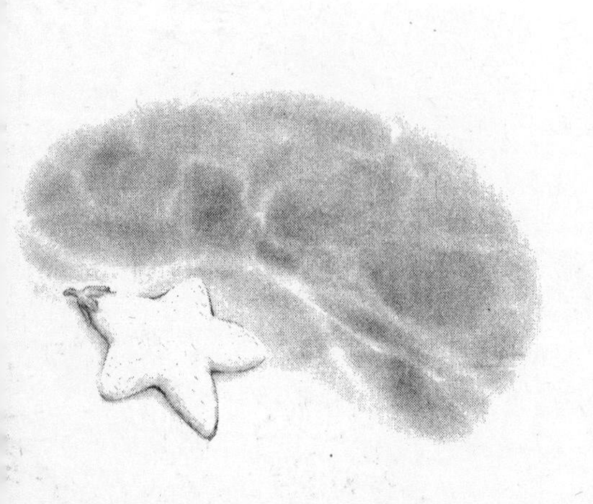

Episode 12
HELPING HAND
10/6

ALICE...! WHERE IS ALICE?!
ALL OF YOU! GO SEARCH FOR ALICE!
I DON'T CARE ANYMORE!! JUST SEIZE SOMEONE!!!!
THIS DOESN'T LOOK TOO GOOD...
SHUFFLE...
GAWRSH!
OFF WITH THEIR HEADS!!
WADDLE WADDLE
LET'S GO FIND ALICE!

THAT QUEEN IS CRAZY!
THE HEARTLESS PROBABLY TOOK ALICE...

I THOUGHT THE HEARTLESS ONLY ATTACKED PEOPLE ON THE SPOT.
I'M NOT SURE...
...BUT SOMETHING MAY BE CONTROLLING THE HEARTLESS.
SOMETHING REALLY EVIL...

AHHH!!
LOOKING FOR ALICE?
YEAH!
DID YOU SEE HER?
NO.
THEN WHAT DO YOU WANT?!
BUT I DO KNOW WHERE THE SHADOW IS.
THIS WAY, IF YOU PLEASE.
WHERE ...?
FWOOM
WHY THE HURRY?
DID YOU KNOW THAT...
BWOH...
LOOOM
...WHEN YOU TURN ON A LIGHT, IT MAKES A SHADOW?

ARE YOU PREPARED FOR THE WORST?
SWISH
SWISH
SWISH
SWISH
IF YOU'RE NOT...THAT'S TOO BAD!
WHOOOOSH

YOU...
YOU TRICKED US!!!
TRICKED YOU? NOTHING OF THE SORT!
THE CHESHIRE CAT IS ALWAYS HERE TO HELP THOSE IN NEED.
FWOOM

HOT, HOT, HOT!
VWOM VWOM VWOM
WAK!
WAAH!
WAAH!
OH, COME ON NOW.

...YOU'LL NEVER BEAT IT LIKE THAT.
WSH
LET ME GIVE YOU SOMETHING YOU'RE MISSING!
SPARKLE
SPARKLE
OH?
SPARKLE

FWOOSH
WHOA!!
ROAST
ROAST
HOT!
HOT!
DONALD!
KNNG
FZH
FIZZLE
?!

THE KEY BEARER...
...SHOULD BE ABLE TO USE A LITTLE MAGIC, RIGHT?
MEEEOW
SORA?!
DID YOU JUST DO THAT?
PUT ME OUT TOO!
TURN
AH-HOO-HOO-HOO-WHEE!

NUMBER
ONE

Episode 13
KEYHOLE

MA—
CHILL
MAGIC?!
THIS IS MAGIC?!
SORA!!
HERE IT COMES!
!
BWOH
BOOM
BOOM
YOINK
YOINK
YOU ASKED FOR IT!
SMIRK...
OUCH...

GZHOOM
MY MAGIC...
URGH ...!
HE JUST BRUSHED IT OFF LIKE IT'S NOTHING!
HEH! HEH!
SLAP
Z-ZSH
WHOA!
AHHHH!
STOMP
STOMP
YOU HAVE TO FOCUS!
WHAT?
SORA!
CURE!

SEE IT IN YOUR MIND!
CONCENTRATE ALL YOUR POWER ON THE TIP OF THE KEYBLADE!
IMAGINE THE ENEMY FREEZING!

THE ENEMY...
...FREEZING!

FREEZE!!!

KRTIK
KRTIK
WE...
GAW... GAWRSH.
KRAK
KRAK
KRAK

CRRRAAASH
OH MY, MY.
YOU DID IT, SORA!

MRK...
WHAT IS IT? WHAT'S GOING ON?
YAWN
SUCH A RACKET. HOW'S A DOORKNOB TO GET ANY SLEEP?
YAAWN...
HOW CAN YOU SLEEP...
...WHEN WE'RE TRYING—

EH?
SOMETHING'S GLOWING...
A KEYHOLE...?
!!

カッ
CLICK
チャ

LET ME SLEEP IN PEACE...
MUMBLE
MUMBLE

WHAT... WAS THAT?
IT SOUNDED LIKE SOMETHING CLOSED WITH A CLICK.

ROLL
?

A-HYUCK, IT'S A GUMMI BLOCK!

GUMMI BLOCK?
YEAH, THEY'RE WHAT WE USE TO BUILD OUR GUMMI SHIP.
YOU'RE RIGHT. I'VE NEVER SEEN THIS KIND OF GUMMI BLOCK BEFORE.
UH, BUT THIS GUMMI AIN'T LIKE OTHERS! NO, SIR!
GIVE IT HERE.

CLAP
CLAP
SPLENDID! YOU'RE QUITE THE HERO.
!
CHESHIRE CAT...
...WHO ARE YOU?
SIMPLY MARVELOUS! YOUR POWER HAS REALLY BLOSSOMED!
I CAN'T WAIT TO SEE WHAT YOU'LL DO NEXT!

SS...
......
IF YOU'RE LOOKING FOR ALICE, YOU WON'T FIND HER HERE.
!
YOU WON'T FIND HER ANYWHERE IN THIS WORLD.
SHE'S GONE WITH THE SHADOWS...INTO THE DARKNESS!

ACCURSED FELINE...
IT NEEDS TO SHUT ITS BIG MOUTH!

WE SHOULD HAVE SENT HIM TO DAVY JONES'S LOCKER AS SOON AS HE REFUSED TO JOIN US!
HA! A LITTLE LATE FOR THAT.

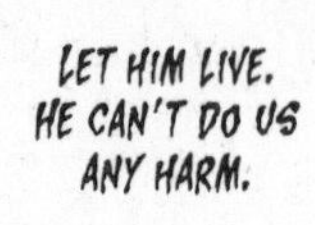
LET HIM LIVE.
HE CAN'T DO US
ANY HARM.

BUT THE BOY
IS A PROBLEM.
HE FOUND
ONE OF THE
KEYHOLES.

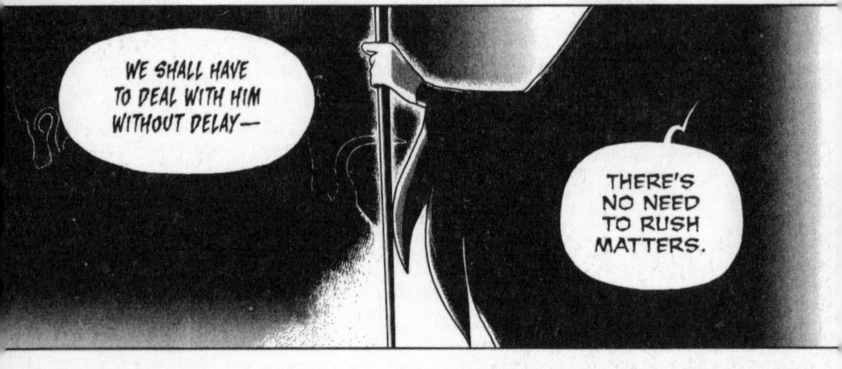
WE SHALL HAVE
TO DEAL WITH HIM
WITHOUT DELAY—
THERE'S
NO NEED
TO RUSH
MATTERS.

IT WILL TAKE HIM AGES TO FIND THE OTHERS.
BESIDES...

FLICK
!
...THE PAWNS ARE ALL FALLING INTO OUR HANDS, ONE BY ONE.

Episode 14

SENTIMENTAL STAR JOURNEY

I COULDN'T FIND ANYONE...
NO ALICE...
...NO KING...
...AND NO RIKU OR KAIRI...

RIKU...
KAIRI...
WHERE ARE YOU?!

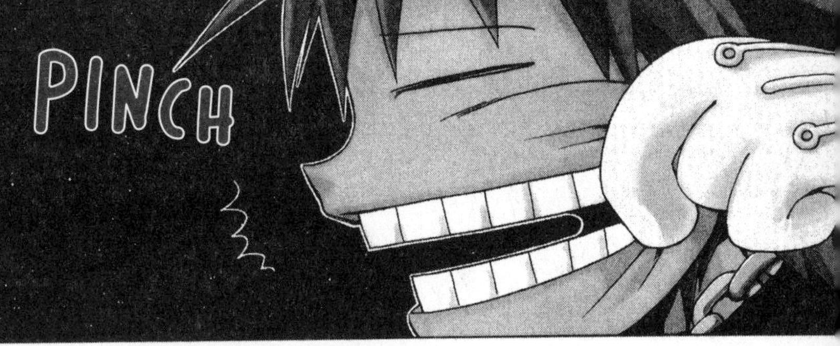
PINCH

DON'T WORRY!
WE'LL FIND 'EM, SORA!
EVERY ONE OF THOSE STARS IS A WORLD WE CAN SEARCH!
...YEAH.
HEY, YOUR FROWN IS GONNA STALL THE ENGINE!
C'MON! SMILE, SMILE!
SQUISH
YOU'RE RIGHT!

TRAVERSE TOWN
OKAY, DONALD! WHERE TO NEXT?
I WANNA BE PILOT!
WAK! NO! STOP THAT!!
ACCESSORIES
OKAY, TALK TO YOU LATER, CID.

PSHHHH
I CAN'T BELIEVE YOU RAMMED US INTO A METEOR!
......
THAT'S THE LAST TIME I'M LETTING YOU FLY OUR SHIP!!

SO, UH... WE'RE BACK...
I... SEE...

WE WANTED TO TALK TO LEON.
LEON'S PROBABLY IN THE SECRET WATERWAY. HE TRAINS THERE ALL THE TIME.

WHO'D'VE THOUGHT THERE'D BE A PLACE LIKE THIS IN THE TOWN SEWERS?

—SO...
...YOU FOUND A KEYHOLE...

Episode 15
THE CHOSEN ONE

YEAH.
THERE WAS THIS LIGHT FROM THE KEYBLADE...
...AND I GUESS IT LOCKED AUTOMATICALLY.
SO, YOU FOUND A KEYHOLE...
ACCORDING TO ANSEM'S REPORT...
...EVERY WORLD AMONG THE STARS HAS A KEYHOLE.
AND EACH ONE LEADS TO THE HEART OF THAT WORLD.
WHAT DO YOU MEAN?

THOSE HEARTS ARE WHAT THE HEARTLESS ARE AFTER.
THEY EXIST WITHIN ALL OF THOSE HEARTS. DARKNESS DOES SOMETHING TO THE WORLD'S CORE, AND THE HEARTLESS APPEAR.

AND WHEN THE HEARTLESS STEAL THE WORLD'S HEART, THAT WORLD DISAPPEARS.
GAWRSH!

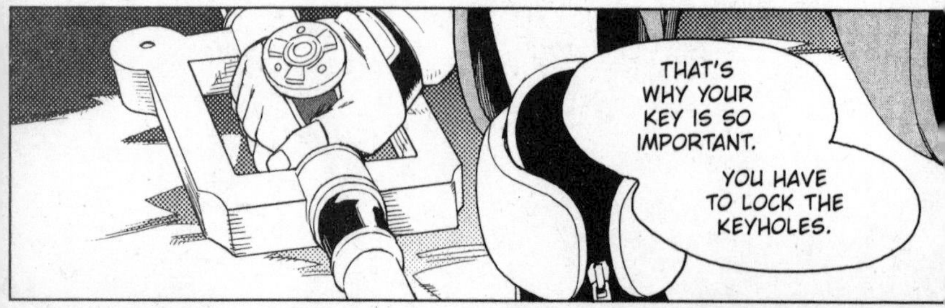
THAT'S WHY YOUR KEY IS SO IMPORTANT.
YOU HAVE TO LOCK THE KEYHOLES.

YOU'VE BEEN CHOSEN BY THE KEYBLADE. YOU'RE THE ONLY ONE WHO CAN DO IT, SORA.

BESIDES, I DOUBT SEEING OTHER WORLDS WOULD BE A WASTE OF YOUR TIME.
SO THAT'S WHY—
B-BUT I'M JUST A—
CLINK
DON'T WORRY.

YOU CAN DO IT...
...SORA.
THIS IS AERITH.
SHE'S A FRIEND OF OURS.
WOULD YOU LIKE SOME ICED TEA?
THANKS.
I ASKED CID TO FIX THE GUMMI SHIP.
REALLY?!
I'LL PASS...
OH YEAH...
WE FOUND THIS GUMMI BLOCK. IT'S NOT LIKE THE OTHERS. ANY IDEA WHAT IT'S FOR?
ASK CID. HE SHOULD KNOW.
GREAT... THANKS.
COME ON, DONALD, GOOFY. LET'S GO!

YOU'RE FLYIN' A GUMMI SHIP, AND YOU DON'T KNOW NOTHIN' ABOUT NAVIGATION GUMMIS?
BUNCHA PINHEADS. INTERSPACE AIN'T NO PLAYGROUND.

ALL RIGHT! I'LL INSTALL IT, SINCE I'M FIXIN' UP THE GUMMI SHIP ANYWAY.
I TOLD YOU TO COME TO ME WHEN YOU NEEDED HELP.
I'M ALWAYS HERE TO LEND A HAND!
REALLY? COOL!

BUT WHILE I'M WORKING ON THAT...
...I'VE GOT SOMETHING I NEED YOU TO DO FOR ME.
RUMMAGE RUMMAGE
HUUUH?!
HAVEN'T YOU HEARD OF "GIVE AND TAKE"?
GOTCHA!!
DON'T MAKE ME ANGRY!

I NEED YOU TO DELIVER THIS BOOK.

WHAT IS IT?
A LOVE DIARY?
NO!!

IT GOES TO THE OLD HOUSE PAST THE THIRD DISTRICT.
LOOK FOR THE BIG FIRE SIGN.
BONG
BONG

Episode 16
THE WIZARD'S HOUSE

GONG
GONG
HELLO?
ANYBODY HOME?

HEY...
CLICK
CREEEAK
THE DOOR'S OPEN.
WOW.

NO ONE'S HERE...
THERE'S SOMETHING ABOUT THIS MUSTY OLD PLACE...
WE HAVE A DELIVERY FOR YOU!
KA-CLUNK
HUH?
RUB RUB
KAIRI?!
HEY.
DOESN'T THIS REMIND YOU OF OUR SECRET SPOT?

PHEW!
KOFF!
WHAT A TERRIBLE LANDING... KOFF, KOFF!
!!
PAT PAT
WELL, WELL. YOU'VE ARRIVED SOONER THAN I EXPECTED.
GASP
SO CID REPAIRED THE BOOK, DID HE? AND QUICKLY TOO!
HUH? WHAT HAPPENED?

MY NAME IS MERLIN. AS YOU CAN SEE, I AM A SORCERER.
YOUR KING HAS REQUESTED THAT I ASSIST YOU.
THE KING?! WHERE IS HE?
WELL NOW, LET ME SEE... THAT'S A GOOD QUESTION.

BUT ONE THING IS CERTAIN...
SWIRL SWIRL
...YOUR KING IS TRYING TO DO SOMETHING ABOUT THE CALAMITY THAT HAS BEFALLEN THE WORLDS...
A-HYUCK!

HE ASKED ME TO TRAIN YOU IN THE ART OF MAGIC.
ME?
YOU'RE STILL USING THE POWER OF THE KEYBLADE INSTINCTIVELY.
BUT YOU MUST LEARN TO CONTROL YOUR POWER, AND USE IT CONSCIOUSLY.
ESPECIALLY YOU, SORA.
NEVER FORGET THAT.

COME BACK ANYTIME YOU NEED ADVICE.
I'M HERE TO HELP.
AND ONE MORE THING...
...IF YOU FIND ANY MISSING PAGES FROM THIS BOOK, PLEASE BRING THEM BACK TO ME.
THE BOOK HAS A WORLD OF ITS OWN, AND IT WOULD BE A SHAME TO LEAVE IT INCOMPLETE.

LOOKS LIKE WE HAVE MORE THINGS TO FIND.
LET'S TAKE IT ONE STEP AT A TIME.
YEAH, ONE STEP AT A TIME!

LUNGE

!!
CLAMP
SHOOT!
SHH...
BASH
?!
SNAP OUT OF IT, SORA. YOU'RE PATHETIC.

NO WAY!!

Episode 17
REUNION

IT TOOK FOREVER TO FIND YOU, SORA.
FSHH
RIKU!!

PINCH
!!
HEY! CUT THAT OUT!
I'M NOT DREAMING THIS TIME, RIGHT?

WE MADE IT TO THE OUTSIDE WORLD.
...WAIT A SECOND— WHERE'S KAIRI?
ISN'T SHE WITH YOU?
WE'RE FREE TO GO WHEREVER WE WANT.
...WELL, DON'T WORRY.
-OOM
AWW...
—WITH ME AROUND, YOU HAVE NOTHING TO WORRY—
HISS...
JUST LEAVE EVERYTHING TO ME.
WE'LL FIND KAIRI SOON ENOUGH.
LOOM...
BASH

LEAVE IT TO WHO?
SHHH..
SORA, WHAT DID YOU—?
HEY, I'VE LEARNED A FEW TRICKS WHILE LOOKING FOR YOU AND KAIRI...
...WITH THE HELP OF MY FRIENDS HERE.
OH, AND GUESS WHAT? SORA'S THE KEYBLADE MASTER. A-HYUCK!
WHO WOULD'VE THOUGHT IT?
AHEM.
......
HMM...

SO, THIS IS CALLED A KEYBLADE?
HUH?!

HEY! GIVE IT BACK!
HMPH.

CATCH.
POOF
!

WHOA, HOW'D YOU DO THAT?!
OHH...
HEY, IT'S YOUR KEYBLADE. SHOULDN'T YOU KNOW?

HUH?
...WELL...

OKAY! SO, YOU'RE COMING WITH US, RIGHT?
WE'VE GOT THIS AWESOME SHIP!

WAIT TILL YOU SEE IT!

WAK!
SORA! YOU'RE NOT THE BOSS HERE!
AW, C'MON! HE'S MY FRIEND!
AND WE FINALLY FOUND EACH OTHER.
RIKU?
RIKU!
HEY...

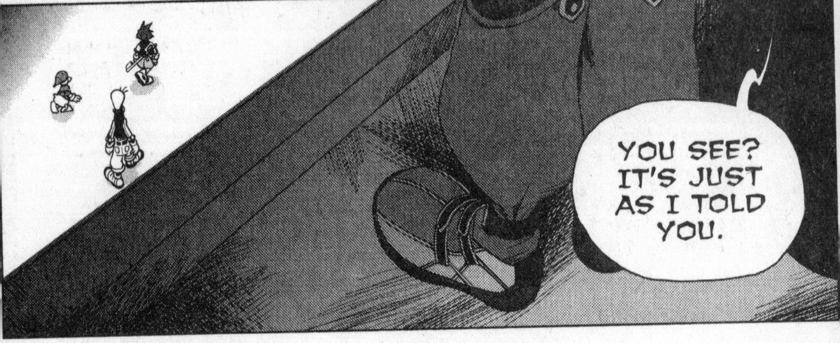
YOU SEE? IT'S JUST AS I TOLD YOU.

WHILE YOU TOILED AWAY TRYING TO FIND YOUR DEAR FRIEND, HE SIMPLY REPLACED YOU WITH SOME NEW COMPANIONS.
GRIT...
EVIDENTLY, HE VALUES THEM FAR MORE THAN HE DOES YOU.

YOU'RE BETTER OFF WITHOUT THAT WRETCHED BOY.
NOW, THINK NO MORE OF HIM AND COME WITH ME.
I'LL HELP YOU FIND WHAT YOU'RE SEARCHING FOR.

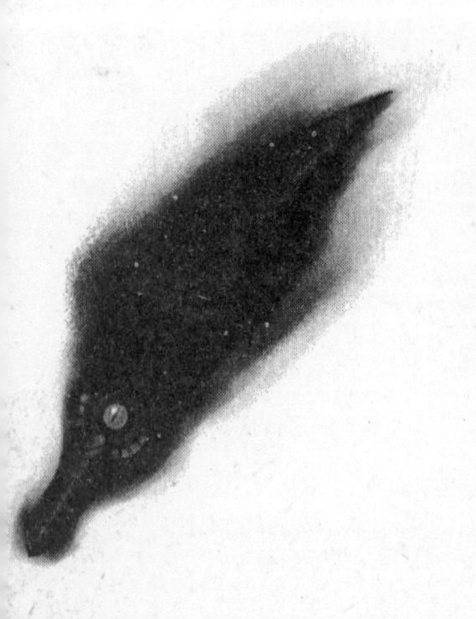

Episode 18
MALEFICENT

NICE GOING. I FINALLY FOUND RIKU...

...AND NOW HE'S GONE AGAIN!
RIKU!

SORA...

CAREFREE
OH WELL.
AT LEAST HE'S OKAY!

WHO KNOWS? MAYBE WE'LL RUN INTO KAIRI SOON TOO.
HUH? WHAT'S WRONG, DONALD?
YOU SURE GOT OVER THAT FAST...
HEY!
A-HYUCK?
ARE YOU GUYS DONE WITH THAT DELIVERY?
THEN COME WITH ME.
WE'RE GOING TO HAVE A STRATEGY MEETING IN OUR SECRET HIDEOUT.
DRESS & SUIT
YOO-HOO, YUFFIE HAS ARRIVED!
OOPS...
GLOOOOM...
IS IT GLOOMY IN HERE, OR WHAT?
MALEFICENT'S BEEN HERE.
WHAT?!

?
MALEFI-WHO?
WE LOST OUR WORLD, THANKS TO HER.
SHE'S A WITCH.
AN EVIL WITCH!
SHE CONTROLS THE HEARTLESS, AND SHE SENT AN ARMY OF THEM TO TAKE OVER.
THESE GUYS WERE JUST KIDS. I ROUNDED 'EM UP AND BROUGHT 'EM HERE.
THAT'S AWFUL!
I HAD NO IDEA...

MALEFICENT IS LOOKING FOR ANSEM'S RESEARCH.
HIS REPORT CONTAINS EVERYTHING THERE IS TO KNOW ABOUT THE HEARTLESS.
SHE WANTS TO USE IT FOR HER EVIL.
WE DON'T KNOW FOR SURE WHAT SHE'S PLOTTING, OR WHY SHE'S USING THE HEARTLESS.
BUT SHE'S ALREADY GOT MOST OF ANSEM'S REPORT.
THEN, LET'S GO!
LET'S FIND THE REST OF THE PAGES!
AND STOP THAT WITCH'S PLAN!
OKAY ?!
GRIN

THE NAVIGATION GUMMI IS INSTALLED, AND YOUR SHIP IS READY TO GO!
GOOD LUCK, BOYS!
WE'RE NOT JUST BEING... USED, ARE WE?
...
SORA?
I WAS THINKING...
MAYBE RIKU'S MAD AT ME...
BUT WHY?
IT WAS BOTHERING HIM!
LOOK! THERE'S OUR NEXT DESTINATION.
HFF...
PUFF...
HFF...
TEP TEP TEP TEP TEP...

PUFF...
HFF...
ZSH
ZSH
ZSH
ZSH
HFF...
HIDE...
AFTER HER!
DON'T LET HER ESCAPE!
ZSH
ZSH
BUT DO TAKE CARE NOT TO HARM HER...
SHE IS OUR DEAR PRINCESS, AFTER ALL...

Episode 19
AGRABAH

HOO-HA-HA!
SOON, I WILL BE FREE OF THE HUMILIATION OF SERVING AS A LOWLY VIZIER.
AGRABAH BELONGS TO THE GREAT JAFAR...HEH-HEH-HEH.
HAVE YOU CAPTURED ALL OF THE CITIZENRY, JAFAR?
BUT OF COURSE...
...MALEFICENT.

AND I'M CERTAIN THAT THE HEARTLESS WILL LOCATE THIS CITY'S KEYHOLE SOON ENOUGH.
VERY WELL.
FLAP
FLAP
AND WHAT OF THE PRINCESS?
BAD NEWS, JAFAR! JASMINE'S GONE!
DISAPPEARED LIKE MAGIC!
HMPH.
THE GIRL IS MORE TROUBLE THAN SHE'S WORTH.
AGRABAH IS FULL OF HOLES...
...FOR RATS TO HIDE IN.
YOU'D BETTER SUCCEED.
WE NEED ALL SEVEN PRINCESSES.
HOP
OF COURSE...

AFTER ALL, THE PRINCESSES ARE THE KEY TO OPENING THE FINAL DOOR.
AND ONCE IT'S OPEN, THE WORLDS WILL BE OURS.
ISN'T THAT RIGHT?
SMIRK...
......
DON'T STEEP YOURSELF IN DARKNESS FOR TOO LONG.
THE HEARTLESS CONSUME THE CARELESS.
SSS...

HMPH...
YOUR CONCERN IS TOUCHING, BUT HARDLY NECESSARY.
......
THANK YOU, ABU.
OO-OO!
I CAN'T BELIEVE JAFAR HAS TAKEN OVER AGRABAH.
IT LOOKS LIKE WE'RE SAFE NOW.
OH NO...
DO YOU THINK ALADDIN IS ALL RIGHT?

HER NAME'S JASMINE. SHE HAS SILKY BLACK HAIR AND BEAUTIFUL EYES THAT JUST PULL YOU IN.

I'M CRAZY ABOUT HER...

...BUT SHE'S A PRINCESS, AND I'M—

AW, SHE COULD NEVER FALL FOR A GUY LIKE ME.
ALADDIN, THAT'S NOT TRUE!
RIGHT, EVERYONE?
YEAH!
A-HYUCK!
YEAH!
BELIEVE IN YOURSELF!
BESIDES, YOU'RE HANDSOME!
OH, STOP THAT...YOU'RE EMBARRASS-ING ME...
JUST HELP US ALREADY!!
SINK SINK...
OH... RIGHT.
HOLD ON A SECOND...
RUB RUB RUB
COME ON OUT, GENIE!

RIKU! CHECK THIS OUT!
THERE'S A CAVE HERE!
120% Value!
All-New Bonus Chapter
BEYOND THE DOOR
SECRET PLACE

オォ…
HOWL
DID YOU HEAR THAT?!
ウオオオオォ
HOOOOWL
!?
SO—
D'YOU THINK SOMETHING'S IN THERE?

RIKU!

HEH...
YOU SCARED?

YOU CAN'T GO IN THERE!
WHAT IF IT'S A MONSTER?!

Y—
YOU BETTER WATCH YOUR STEP, OKAY! IT'S DARK!

THAT HURTS!
HOOOOOWL
WHOA!
BONK
OW!
YEAH. WATCH YOUR HEAD TOO.

LET'S GO.

HOWL

WHOA...
COOL!!

HOOOWL
WHOA!
HOWL

IT'S THE WIND.
HUH?
HOWL
HOWL
IT'S THE WIND. THAT'S WHAT'S MAKING THOSE MONSTER SOUNDS.

OOHHH...

I CAN SEE THE SKY!

A DOOR...?

HEY!
LET'S MAKE THIS OUR SECRET HIDEOUT!

GOOD IDEA, HUH?!
GLOW...

YEAH.

DON'T TELL ANYONE!
IT'S OUR SECRET PLACE!

WHERE DOES THAT DOOR LEAD?

SOMEDAY, I'M GOING TO GET AWAY FROM THIS WORLD...

...AND SEE WHAT'S BEYOND THAT DOOR.

I SHOULD HAVE...
...TRIED THAT PAOPU FRUIT THING.

WHATEVER BRINGS YOU HERE, CHILD?

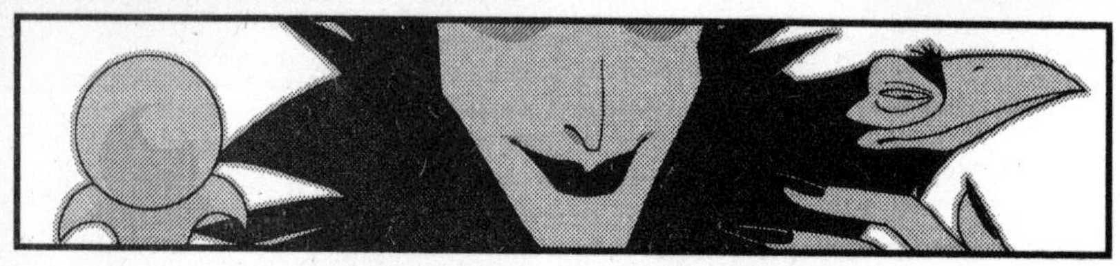

COME TO MY CASTLE...
...AND TELL ME ALL ABOUT IT.

Episode 20

THE GENIE OF THE LAMP

ALL RIGHT, NOW FOR MY FIRST WISH!
PUFF PUFF PUFF
SAVE THEM FROM THE QUICKSAND!
RRRAAAAAH

TA-DAAAH!!
HEY, HEY, HEY!
HONK HONK HONK!
RUB-A-DUB-DUB THE LAMP AND HAVE YOUR DEAREST WISHES GRANTED!
BY THE ONE, THE ONLY GENIE OF THE LAMP!
TODAY'S WINNER IS...ALADDIN! CONGRATULATIONS!
YOU CAN SAVE THE INTRODUCTION!
WISH NUMBER ONE, COMING RIGHT UP!
SNAP OF THE FINGERS, AND BOOM!
Z-ZSHHH

HARDLY ANYONE EVER COMES THROUGH HERE, NOT EVEN CARAVANS.
YOU'RE LUCKY I HAPPENED TO PASS BY.
THANKS. YOU'RE A LIFESAVER.
ALADDIN, WHAT'RE YOU DOING OUT HERE?
IN THIS DESERT...
ME?
WHAT ARE YOU GUYS DOING HERE, ANYWAY?
A-HYUCK!
WE JUMPED OFF OUR GUMMI SHIP AND GOT CAUGHT IN THE QUICKS—
I'M HUNTING LEGENDARY TREASURE.
JUST PAID A VISIT TO THE CAVE OF WONDERS.
THAT'S WHERE I FOUND THIS LAMP!

AND THAT'S WHERE I COME IN! I'M HERE TO GRANT MY MASTER ANY THREE WISHES! ♡
PLEASE CALL ME GENIE! ♡
SO, YOU LUCKY LITTLE MASTER, YOU...
...YOU HAVE TWO—COUNT 'EM—TWO WISHES LEFT!
YOU CAN MAKE ANY WISH COME TRUE?
I WONDER IF HE CAN FIND THE KING...
NO WAY!
SO WHAT'LL IT BE?
HMM...
HOW ABOUT MAKING ME A FABULOUSLY WEALTHY PRINCE?
OOOH! MONEY! ROYALTY! FAME! WHY DIDN'T I THINK OF THAT?
AH, ALMOST. THERE ARE A FEW PROVISOS...
WAHEY!

I THINK I'LL PUT THAT ON HOLD UNTIL WE REACH AGRABAH.
NO, WAIT.
OH?
THEN I WANT TO BECOME A PRINCE...
...SO THAT I CAN PROPOSE TO JASMINE...
WAY TO GO, ALADDIN!
WOO-HOO!
COME ON, LAY OFF...
NO PROBLEM!
THAT'LL GIVE ME MORE TIME TO ENJOY THE FRESH AIR!
BREATHE IN, BREATHE OUT...
IT'S ALWAYS THREE WISHES, THEN BACK TO MY PORTABLE PRISON!
I'M LUCKY TO SEE THE LIGHT OF DAY EVERY CENTURY OR TWO...
PHE-NOMENAL COSMIC POWERS!
ITTY-BITTY LIVING SPACE.
GUESS YOU DON'T GET OUT MUCH, HUH?
COMES WITH THE JOB.

THAT'S TOUGH...
...
SAY, GENIE!
IF I WISHED FOR YOUR FREEDOM...
...WOULD YOU BE RELEASED FROM THE LAMP?
AW, THANKS, AL.
EVEN IF YOU DON'T MEAN IT, IT'S THE THOUGHT THAT COUNTS.
WHOOSH..
HOO KEEKEE SCREEHEE! (...ABOUT JASMINE!)
SCREE SCREEK CREEE! (I HAVE TO TELL ALADDIN...)

Episode 21
DEVIL'S
GRIN

WHOOOOSH
ARE YOU GUYS GOING TO AGRABAH TOO?
IF YOU ASK GENIE, IT'LL ONLY TAKE A MINUTE!
UM, I DON'T THINK THAT'S A VERY SMART THING TO USE YOUR WISH ON, ALADDIN...
THINK BEFORE YOU WISH...
IT'S A LITTLE FAR FROM HERE, BUT...
OH!
HUH?
SKIRREEHEEN!
(ALADDIN!)
WHOOSH
LUNGE
KONK
BRAKE

THIS HERE...
...IS MY PARTNER, ABU.
AND THAT'S THE MAGIC CARPET.
HEY, ABU, KNOCK IT OFF!
GREAT! WE CAN RIDE THIS TO AGRABAH!
BOING
ABU!
HOO HOO!
SKREEHEE!
(THERE'S NO TIME!)
KREE HOO HOO SKREEREE!!
(JASMINE'S BEEN KIDNAPPED!!)

MMF...
MMMFF!
MY DEEPEST APOLOGIES, PRINCESS JASMINE, FOR THE LESS THAN HOSPITABLE TREATMENT.
UMPH!!!
HEY, JAFAR, DO YOU THINK THAT STREET RAT WILL COME RESCUE HER?

OF COURSE HE'LL COME...
HMM...
...WITH LAMP IN HAND.
THAT'S WHY WE SET THAT MONKEY LOOSE.
YOU'RE SO EVIL, JAFAR.
HAHA HA
GYAH HA! GYAH HA HA HA HA!
HOO HEH HEH HEH HEH
ALADDIN, IT'S A TRAP! PLEASE STAY AWAY...

WITH THAT MAGIC LAMP...AND THE POWERS OF DARKNESS...
...I WILL RULE THE WORLD— I WILL RULE EVERYTHING!!!

......
IT SEEMS THEY'VE ARRIVED! HA-HA-HA...
WHOOSH

ZSH
JAFAR!!!

YOUR EVILDOING STOPS HERE!
GIVE BACK JASMINE!

OOPS... SORRY.
HEY... I WAS GONNA SAY THAT...

FLAP
FLAP
TOO LATE.
PWAH!
ALADDIN! STAY AWAY!
IT'S A TRAP!

THE LAMP HAS A NEW MASTER NOW.
WHAT?
OH NO!
GO, HEARTLESS.
ENTERTAIN OUR GUESTS.

Episode 22
THE PRICE OF GREED

CLASH
DON'T LET THEM SCARE YOU, GOOFY!
CLANK
GAWRSH!
WHOA!!
ALADDIN!
HERE...
LET'S PUT A LID ON THE NOISY PRINCESS.
......!!
KRIK
KAPOP
SKITTER SKITTER

JASMINE!
!!!
SHNK
WAAAH!!

CLATTER
CLATTER
NOW THEN...

MY FIRST WISH...
...GENIE.
SHOW ME THE KEYHOLE!
AYE-AYE, SIR!
ONE RUB OF THE LAMP, AND I COME RUNNING! CAREFUL! YOU MIGHT GET HIT BY CHARGING GENIES!
POOOOF
THIS IS YOUR SECOND WISH, AL! AND DON'T TRY TO TELL ME THAT...
I...
...DON'T THINK YOU'RE HIM.
THIS WAY.
LET'S HURRY!
FSHHH
HFF...
HFF...
ABU! WHAT ARE YOU DOING?!
SORA?!

ZHRRN...
?!
WHAT'S THAT?
IT'S STRANGE...
...BUT I THINK THE KEYBLADE IS TELLING ME TO GO THIS WAY!
I WOULD EXPECT NOTHING LESS OF AN ALL-POWERFUL GENIE.
WITH YOUR POWERS, WE COULD RULE THE WORLD TOGETHER!
GIMME A BREAK, MASTER.
PATTER PATTER...
MWAH-HA-HA!
YOU WOULD LEAVE US, JAFAR?

MALEFICENT!
THAT WAS MERELY JEST...
LEAVE IF YOU WISH.
I CAN EASILY FIND A REPLACE-MENT.
......

...I CAN JOKE TOO.
SKITTER
SKITTER
......!
......!!
I'LL BE TAKING THE PRINCESS.
MPH!

WAIT!!!

UGH ...
JAFAR! GIVE JASMINE BACK!
TAK
TAK
I'M AFRAID I CAN'T DO THAT.
...!!
ARE YOU MALEFICENT?
SS...
JASMINE!!
!

WHF
!!

GENIE!
YOU GOTTA SAVE JASMINE!
...!
...!
WHERE DID YOU TAKE HER?!
AL...

IT PAINS ME TO INFORM YOU, BUT I AM THE GENIE'S MASTER NOW.

NO!
GENIE...
OOH, I JUST HAD THE MOST ENTERTAINING IDEA!
...I WANT YOU TO CRUSH THESE STREET RATS.

YOU HEARD ME. I COMMAND YOU TO TEACH THEM WHAT PAIN IS.
DON'T LISTEN TO HIM, GENIE!
......
THAT'S A STUPID WISH!
THE ONE WITH THE LAMP CALLS THE SHOTS...
SORRY, AL.
GENIE, NO!

WAAH-HA-HA-HA!
YESSS!
WHAT'S WRONG WITH YOU? YOU'RE SUPPOSED TO HIT THEM!
EVERY-ONE GET AWAY!
ZAP ZAP BOOM BOOM
DON'T LET ME HIT YOU!
THE NEXT ONE'S GOING THAT WAY!
KABOOM
POOF POOF
A-HYUCK!
SORRY, I DIDN'T MEAN TO!
ZAP
ZAP
GWAAH!!!
YOU'RE TOO SOFT, GENIE!
LET ME SHOW YOU HOW IT'S DONE!

GENIE! MY FINAL WISH!
I WANT YOU TO MAKE ME AN ALL-POWERFUL GENIE!

POOF

HAAAAA-HA-HA-HA-HA-HA-HA-HAA!!
YES! THE POWER! THE ABSOLUTE POWER!!
WITH THIS POWER, THE UNIVERSE IS MINE TO COMMAND!!
I'LL SHOW YOU, MALEFICENT.
FLAP

NOW THEN...
...I'LL START BY TAKING OUT THE TRASH.
TIME TO DISAPPEAR, WORMS!!
NO, YOU'RE THE ONE WHO'S GOING TO DISAPPEAR, JAFAR.

JAFAR! BACK TO YOUR LAMP!

WHAT...
...DID YOU SAY?
THE ONE WITH THE LAMP CALLS THE SHOTS!
NO!

AAAAA-
AAAAHH!!!

60
10
F
CHIP 'N' DALE
Episode 23
THE LAST WISH

THIS... IS THE FATE OF A GENIE?!
JAFAR! LET GO OF ME!
CLAMP
AAAHH!!!
NO... IMPOSSIBLE...
THIS CAN'T BE HAPPENING!!

POP
LIKE YOUR NEW HOME?
WAAH! HOW DID THIS HAPPEN?!
GET YOUR BLASTED BEAK OUT OF MY FACE!
FLUTTER
FLUTTER
RUSTLE
HUH?
THIS IS...
...PART OF ANSEM'S REPORT!
SORA!
ARGH!

SORA, YOU LITTLE GENIUS, YOU!!!
WHO'DA THOUGHT YOU COULD USE YOUR BRAIN?!
DID YOU SAY SOME-THING?
YOINK
I'M GONNA TAKE THIS LAMP...
WHOOSH
...AND BURY IT! HA!
SHFF
SHFF
LET ME OUT!
BURY IT?!

SPARKLE
SPARKLE...

SPARKLE
SPARKLE
OH YEAH! WE HAVE TO SEAL THE KEYHOLE!
FLASH
FSHHH
CLICK
OKAY, THAT SHOULD DO IT.
RUMBLE...
HUH?

ZOOM

UH-OH...

AA-HOO-HOO-HOO-WHEE-EEE!

GOOFY!!!

!!

GENIE!
SAVE HIM! HURRY!!
THAT'LL BE YOUR SECOND WISH.
I KNOW!
FLOAT
A-HYUCK!
THANKS, ALADDIN.
I THOUGHT I WAS A GONER...

HEY... IT JUST SLIPPED OUT OF MY MOUTH...
PLEASE! TAKE ME WITH YOU TO THIS OTHER WORLD!!
I'M SORRY, BUT WE CAN'T.
IT'S AGAINST THE RULES.
WE CAN'T TAKE SOMEON FROM THIS WO TO A DIFFERE ONE.
...
YEAH, I GUESS IT'S NOT FAIR OF ME TO IMPOSE.
I'M SORRY.
POOR GUY...
...
UH, EARTH TO AL.
HELLO? YOU STILL HAVE ONE WISH LEFT.

LOOK, JUST SAY THE WORD. ASK ME TO FIND JASMINE FOR YOU.
BUT, GENIE...
OKAY, HERE'S MY FINAL WISH.

I WISH... FOR YOUR FREEDOM, GENIE.

FLAAAASH
WHAT?

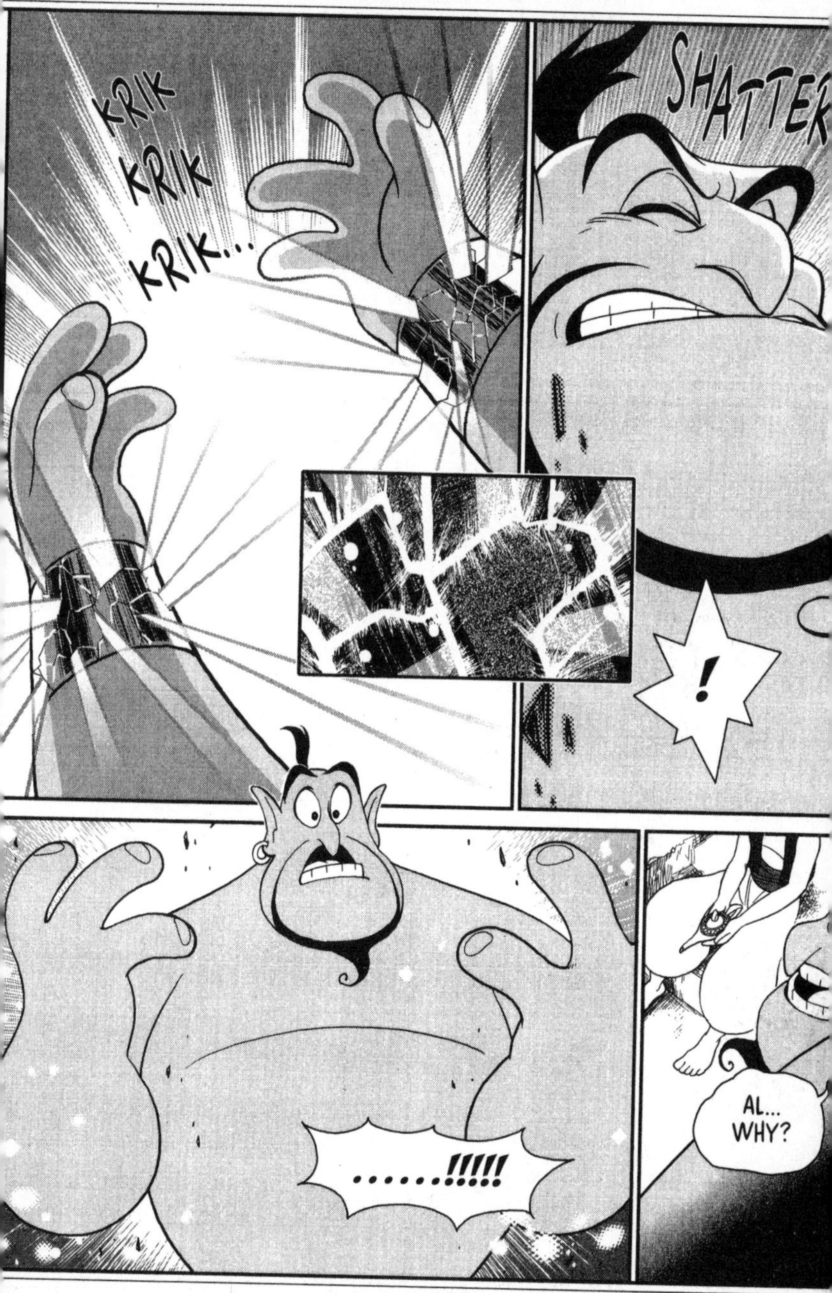
KRIK
KRIK
KRIK...
SHATTER
!
......!!!!!
AL...
WHY?

HEY.
A DEAL'S A DEAL, GENIE.

ERK!
LUNGE
!
BUT WHY WOULD YOU...?

YOU'RE MY BEST FRIEND!

WE'LL FIND JASMINE. I PROMISE.
JUST YOU WAIT.
I'M NOT TIED TO THE LAMP ANYMORE.
BUT YOU CAN STILL USE IT TO CALL ME ANYTIME.
HERE, TAKE THIS.
I WANT TO HELP YOU SAVE MY PAL'S GIRLFRIEND!

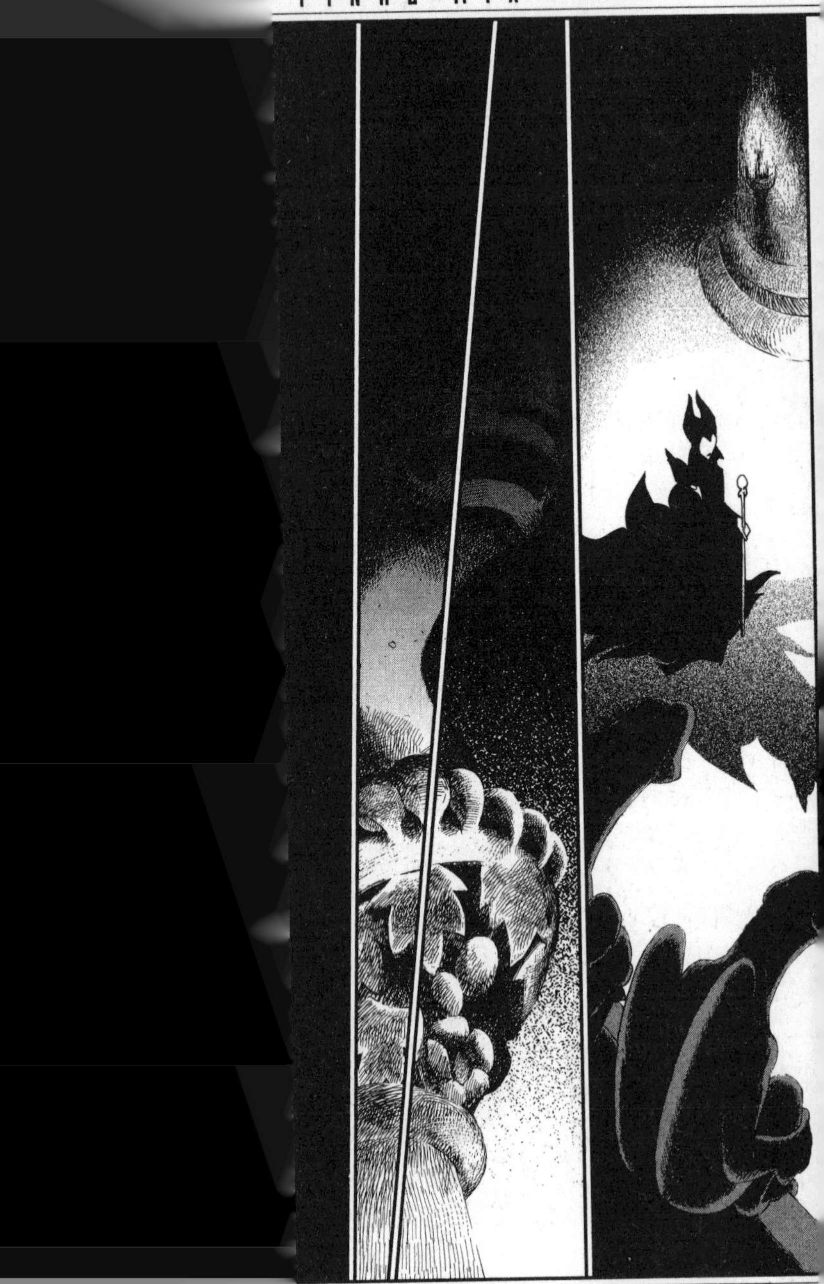

HOW ARE YOU FEELING?

Episode 24
OLYMPUS COLISEUM

IT'S SO DARK IN THERE...
WHY DON'T YOU TURN ON A LIGHT?
I FEEL MORE COMFORTABLE IN THE DARK.
DO AS YOU PLEASE.
LIFT
IT IS YOUR ROOM, AFTER ALL.
ARE YOU READY TO JOIN OUR CAUSE?

...I HAVE NO IDEA WHAT YOU GUYS ARE UP TO.

BUT I'LL PLAY ALONG FOR NOW.

YOU'VE GOTTEN AWFULLY ATTACHED.
HADES...
YOU BETTER NOT BE HIDING SOMETHING FROM THE REST OF US.
WHAT CAN HE DO FOR YOU, ANYWAY? HE'S JUST A SNOT-NOSED KID.
THE COLD SHOUL-DER, EH?
OH WELL...
I'LL JUST GO AHEAD AND THROW MY OWN LITTLE PARTY.
SHE'S NOT THE ONLY ONE WHO CAN KEEP SECRETS.

GREAT, NOW WE HAVE EVEN MORE THINGS TO FIND.
WHY DON'T WE JUST PUT UP A SIGN ON THE SHIP THAT SAYS "LOST AND FOUND CENTER"?
...THAT'S NOT FUNNY
WE'RE OUT SEARCHING ANYWAY, SO WHY NOT HELP THEM TOO?
I'M ABOUT TO FORGET WHAT WE'RE LOOKING FOR IN THE FIRST PLACE!
BEEP
BEEP
HEY...
WHAT'S THIS?
YO, HOW'S IT GOIN'?
PUSH ME!
?!
I'VE NEVER SEEN THIS BUTTON BEFORE.
HOW'S THE QUEST?
WAK!

CID?!
WHEN DID YOU—?!
Heh-heh-heh!
I installed it during the repair.
Didn't Chip 'n' Dale tell you?
DOESN'T ANYBODY EVER ASK ME?!
Say what?
SORRY, DONALD'S A LITTLE ON EDGE RIGHT NOW.
We sealed Agrabah's Keyhole...
...and found a sheet from Ansem's report.
GOOD JOB, KIDS!
BUT I CAN'T READ WHAT'S WRITTEN IN THE REPORT.
Okay, fax it to me.
We'll get it decoded.
FAX?!
VNNNNN
Pretty handy, eh?
LEON AND THE OTHERS ARE GATHERING INFO TOO.
IT'S DEFINITELY LOOKIN' LIKE MALEFICENT IS UP TO SOMETHING.

The Heartless are kidnapping specific people from the different worlds.
WE SAW MALEFICENT.
SHE KIDNAPPED A GIRL RIGHT FROM UNDER OUR NOSES.
WHAT?
I see...
Well, you guys just keep on sealing them Keyholes.
ROGER THAT!
THERE'S OUR NEXT DESTINATION!

WOW...
THAT GATE IS HUGE!
LET'S SEE...
OLYMPUS COLISEUM...
...IS WHERE WARRIORS FROM ALL AROUND COME TO TEST THEIR SKILL IN THE GAMES. ...IS WHAT IT SAYS RIGHT HERE.
SNORT
THE GAMES?!!
......

WE HAVE NO TIME TO PLAY GAMES, SORA!
INFORMATION
AWW, COME ON—LET'S JUST TAKE A PEEK!
RULES
EXCUSE ME...
GOOD TIMING. GIVE ME A HAND, WILL YA?
RULES
MOVE THAT PEDESTAL OVER THERE FOR ME.
WHAT?
WELL, OKAY...I GUESS.
NOW YOU'RE HELPING WITH HIS SPRING CLEANING!
A-HYUCK A-HYUCK!
SHUT UP!
IT WEIGHS...
...A TON!!

ARGH...
PUSH...
GRRRRRAAAH!!
IT'S WAY TOO HEAVY!
WHAT? TOO HEAVY?
HERC! SINCE WHEN HAVE YOU BEEN SUCH A LITTLE—
WHIRL
......
OH. WRONG GUY. WHAT'RE YOU DOING HERE?
GET LOST.
UMM... I WANT TO ENTER THE GAMES.
SORA!!
WHAT?
A PIP-SQUEAK LIKE YOU?
A LITTLE RUNT WHO CAN'T EVEN MOVE A PEDESTAL?!

LISTEN UP! THIS HERE'S THE WORLD-FAMOUS COLISEUM!
HEROES ONLY!
IF YOU WANNA BE IN THE GAMES, THEN YOU GOTTA BRING ME AN ENTRY PASS!
NOT THAT YOU'LL EVER GET ONE.
YOU CAN'T EVEN MOVE A PEDESTAL LIKE THIS...
URGH...
ARGH...
......
ANYHOW, MY HANDS ARE FULL ENOUGH ALREADY! SO RUN ALONG, PIP-SQUEAKS!
WHAT'S YOUR PROBLEM, GOAT-MAN?!
YOU CAN'T TREAT ME LIKE A KID!
YEAH! YOU'VE GOT HEROES STANDING RIGHT IN FRONT OF YOU.
HERE'S A REAL HERO CHOSEN BY THE KEYBLADE!
THAT'S RIGHT!
A-HYUCK!
YOU TELL HIM, DONALD!
RATHER A STUBBORN OLD GOAT, WOULDN'T YOU SAY?
IGNORING A PROMISING YOUNG HOPEFUL LIKE YOURSELF.

I KNOW HERCULES IS HIS PRIZE PUPIL, BUT COME ON!
HE'S PUTTING ALL HIS EGGS IN ONE BASKET. WHAT HAPPENS WHEN HERCULES IS GONE, AM I RIGHT?
SORRY. I WAS JUST TALKING TO MYSELF.
......
AND WHO ARE YOU?
LET ME GUESS. YOU WANT TO ENTER THE GAMES, RIGHT? I CAN SEE IT IN YOUR EYES.
THOSE ARE THE EYES OF A TRUE HERO!
SO GET A LOAD OF THIS.
CAN I REALLY HAVE THIS?

WHAT?!!
NO WAY... HOW'D YOU GET THIS?
CAN WE ENTER THE GAMES NOW?
WELL...
I GUESS SO.
...BUT...
...FIRST YOU NEED SOME TRAINING, COURTESY OF YOURS TRULY!!
WHEN I'M THROUGH WITH YOU, YOUR MUSCLES WILL HAVE MUSCLES!
WH-WHAT?
CONVENIENT THAT THE KID WITH THE KEYBLADE IS HERE.
YOU'LL BE FIGHTING THAT LITTLE PUNK IN THE TOURNAMENT. DON'T BLOW IT. JUST TAKE HIM OUT.

I'M NOT AFRAID OF THE LITTLE SHORTY.
YOU JUST KEEP YOUR OPINIONS TO YOURSELF, AND HOLD UP YOUR END OF THE BARGAIN, CAPICHE?
SORRY, BUT MY CONTRACT ONLY SAYS TO KILL HERCULES.
I KNOW! I WROTE THE CONTRACT!
JUST GET RID OF THE KID WHILE YOU'RE AT IT!
THINK OF IT AS AN ADDED SERVICE OPTION.
HADES, THE GREAT GOD OF THE UNDERWORLD, IS AFRAID OF A KID?

GEEZ.
STIFFER THAN THE STIFFS BACK HOME.

STILL...
GRRRR...
...SUCKERS LIKE HIM ARE HARD TO COME BY.
RELAX SHOULDERS, CHIN TO YOUR CHEST!
WHIP
WHY ARE THERE THUMBTACKS IN MY SHOES?!

Episode 25
WHAT IT MEANS TO BE A HERO

THE STRONGEST!
THE KINDEST!
ALWAYS SHOWS UP IN THE NICK OF TIME!
AND EVEN GOOD-LOOKING!
YES! THAT'S WHAT IT MEANS TO BE A HERO!

YOU AIN'T HEROES YET, BUT YOU'RE DOING GOOD FOR ROOKIES.
I HAVEN'T ENJOYED COACHING THIS MUCH IN A LONG TIME.
HOW LONG HAVE WE BEEN AT THIS?
A-HYUCK!
TWO HOURS AND FORTY MINUTES...
AFTER ALL THAT TRAINING, WE SHOULD SEE...
...SOME RESULTS.
WOBBLE WOBBLE...
HERO LEVEL
BUT IT TAKES MORE THAN STRONG MUSCLES TO MAKE A TRUE HERO.
IT TAKES HEART!
THUMP!
TO BE A HERO, YOU NEED A STRONG HEART.
SO HOW DO I GET A STRONG HEART?
YOU'LL HAVE TO FIND THAT OUT FOR YOURSELF.

HERC!
HEY, PHIL.
I'M DONE CLEANING THE COLISEUM TOILETS.
LET ME INTRODUCE YOU.
THIS IS THE COLISEUM'S REIGNING CHAMP, THE CELEBRATED HERO—TRAINED BY YOURS TRULY—
HERCULES!
...CLEANING TOILETS?!
SHOCK
YEAH.
THAT'S WHAT YOU ASKED ME TO DO.
BWAH-HA-HA-HA! I CAN'T BELIEVE I MADE A HERO CLEAN TOILETS.
PUMP PUMP
TREMBLE TREMBLE
AND I WAS LOOKING AT THE ENTRY LIST.
I NOTICED THERE ARE A LOT OF SUSPICIOUS CHARACTERS COMPETING THIS TIME AROUND.
SOMEONE MUST BE SCALPING ENTRY PASSES.

THE STRONGEST, KINDEST, AND BEST-LOOKING HERO AROUND ...
...HERCULES.
SMASH
IF IT WEREN'T FOR THAT YUTZ, I WOULD BE RUNNING THIS WORLD BY NOW!
FWOOOM
WHOOPS. A RULER NEEDS TO STAY COOL.
GRAR!

THE PIECES ARE ALL IN PLACE.

THE CHUMP WITH THE SWORD WILL TAKE OUT BOTH THE KEYBLADE KID AND HERCULES.
CLUNK
CLUNK
AND ONCE HERCULES IS OUT OF THE PICTURE, THE REST IS EASY.

I'LL GET THAT KEYBLADE...
...AND USE IT TO RELEASE THE TITANS FROM THEIR PRISON!
THE KEYBLADE CAN OPEN DOORS TO WHOLE WORLDS.
IT'D BE A CAKEWALK TO OPEN A MEASLY LITTLE PRISON LOCK.
BINK
AND THEN...
...I, HADES, WILL BE RULER OF THE COSMOS!!
......
I'M TALKING TO MYSELF MORE AND MORE THES DAYS.

BASH
BWOOH
KA-KHNG
GRAH!
GOOD JOB, KID!
GET 'EM!
HIYAH!
WHOOOOOSH
Winner— Team Sora!
WAAAAHH
ALL RIGHT, WE'RE WINNING OUR WAY UP THE LADDER!
WAITING ROOM
LET'S KEEP THIS STREAK GOING!
?
WHAT'S THE MATTER?

ISN'T IT WEIRD THAT THERE ARE HEARTLESS IN THE TOURNAMENT?
THIS WORLD'S KEYHOLE MUST BE OPEN TOO.
WE HAVE TO FIND IT.
WHAT ARE YOU GUYS WHISPERING ABOUT?
WE HAVE TO GET READY FOR OUR NEXT FIGHT.
THE NEXT OPPONENT IS...
WHUD

YOU'RE NO MATCH FOR ME.

KID!!

YOU'RE JUST A KID. ...WHAT IS HADES UP TO?

I SEE. I THOUGHT THAT WAS A TOY YOU WERE SWINGING AROUND.

!

SHOOM...

UGH...
WHY IS IT THAT NONE OF MY THROWAWAY PAWNS...
...ARE EVER HAPPY MINDING THEIR OWN BUSINESS?
GRRAWRR
UGH!
!!
STUNNED
GRAR

KA
POW
YOWL
HERC!
STRAIN STRAIN STRAIN...
PHIL, GET THEM OUT OF HERE!
HURRY!
BE CAREFUL, HERCULES!
HFF HFF...
WHEW, THAT WAS CLOSE! THAT WAS CERBERUS, THE GUARDIAN OF THE UNDERWORLD.
HERC SHOULD FINISH IT OFF IN A SECOND OR TWO...
OH NO...

WHACK
WHAM WHAM WHAM
SHOOM
...WILL HERC BE OKAY ON HIS OWN?
DRAG DRAG
BASH
HERC!
CLINK
THIS AIN'T JUST SOME MATCH. THIS IS FOR REAL!
!
WHERE ARE YOU GOING, KID?
I'M GOING TO HELP HERCULES.
WHAT?!
I KNOW! I'M NOT AFRAID.

YOU CAN DECIDE IF I'M HERO MATERIAL OR NOT.
!
WHY D'YOU ALWAYS HAFTA SHOW OFF, SORA?
WE'RE GOIN' WITH YOU.
A-HYUCK!

F...
HFF...

HERCULES!
SORA!

WE'LL TAKE IT FROM HERE!

HEY, KID! I GOT TWO WORDS OF ADVICE FOR YOU!
ATTACK!
TWO WORDS ??

COME ON OUT, GENIE!

CAFÉ DE AERITH

FINAL MIX JUICE

MR. FANCY